Mess MONsters

illustrated by **Piers Harper**

meadowside
CHILDREN'S BOOKS

One day Mummy said
That my room was a mess,
And because it's untidy
She suffers from stress.

I said,

"I need the mess,
It's better that way,
If I tidied my room
I just wouldn't play!"

What I didn't know,

Was that under my bed,

Was a big gang of monsters

Who'd heard what I'd said.

A Claw

then a paw

then a **hORrible** sight,

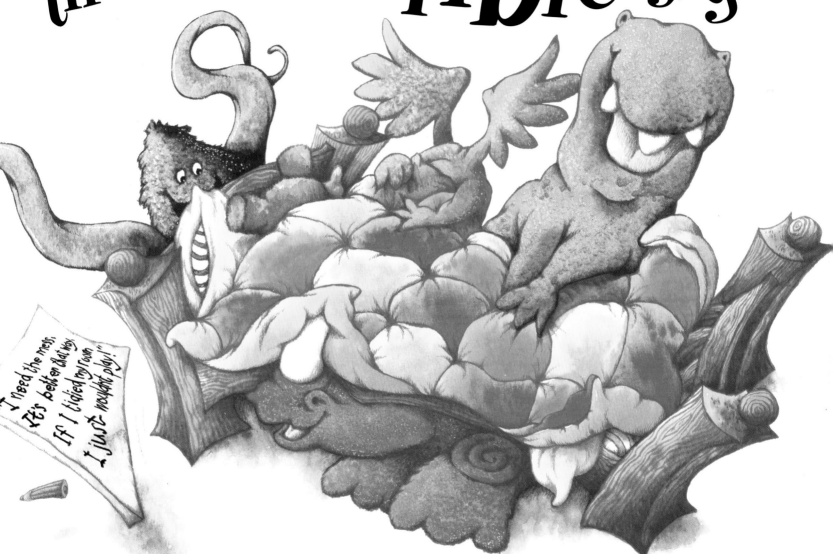

as **masses** of monsters, **crawled** into the light!

These **Terrible** monsters

Made terrible noise,

As they **Crashed**

And they **Smashed** up all of my toys.

They **broke** all my games,

And before I was ready,

They **jumped** on my cars

And **Clobbered** poor Teddy.

They leapt on my bed
And they **ch^ewed** all the sheets,

Then **squashed** all my clothes
With their **BIG** smelly feet.

They **banged** down their tails
So the whole bedroom **shook**,

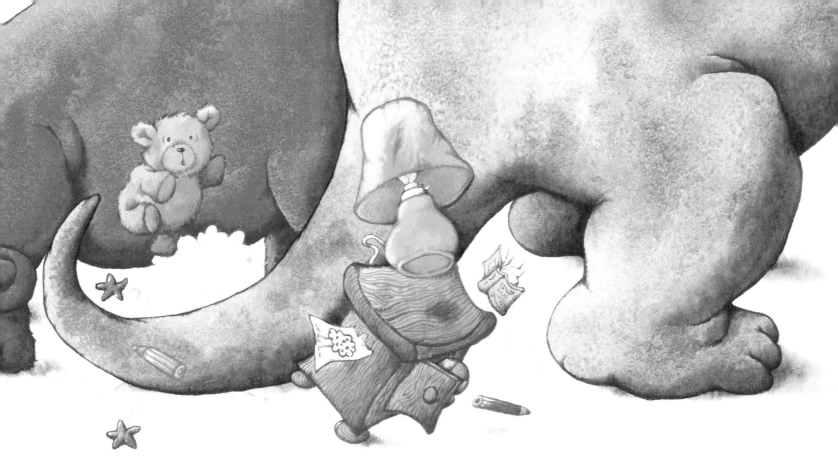

Then **stomped** on my cushions
And **ate** all my books.

Enough was enough!

So I shouted,

Oi!

Stop!

They're MY things
you're breaking.

I want you to stop!"

"I'll clean and I'll tidy!

I'll sweep up all day!

If that's what is needed
To send you away."
"You'll go if it's clean.
You don't like it that way.
You only like mess,

(That's what
Mummy
would say")

The horrible monsters
Frowned at each other.
They knew that they'd lose
In a fight with MY mother!

They panicked and ran

When they heard what I said,

Back to the mess,

At the end of my bed.

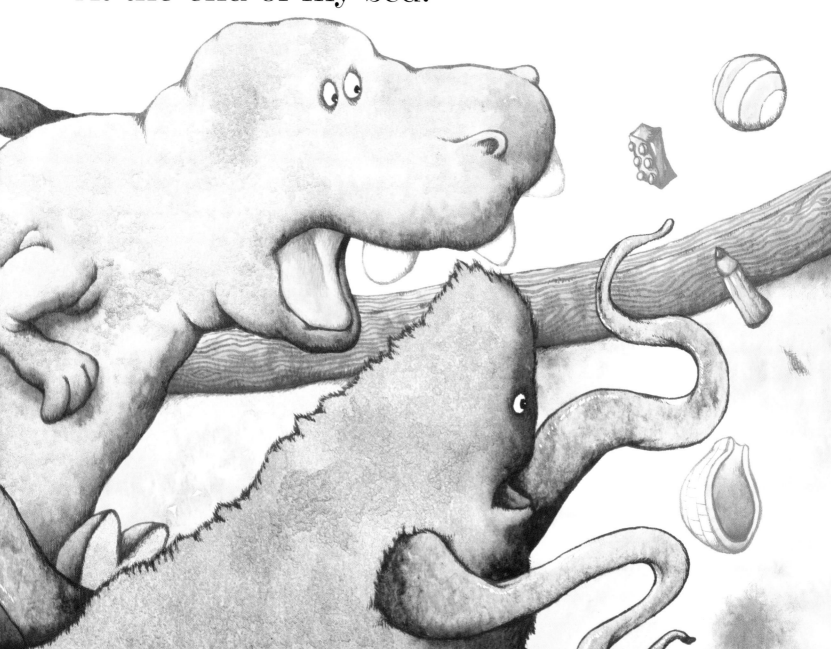

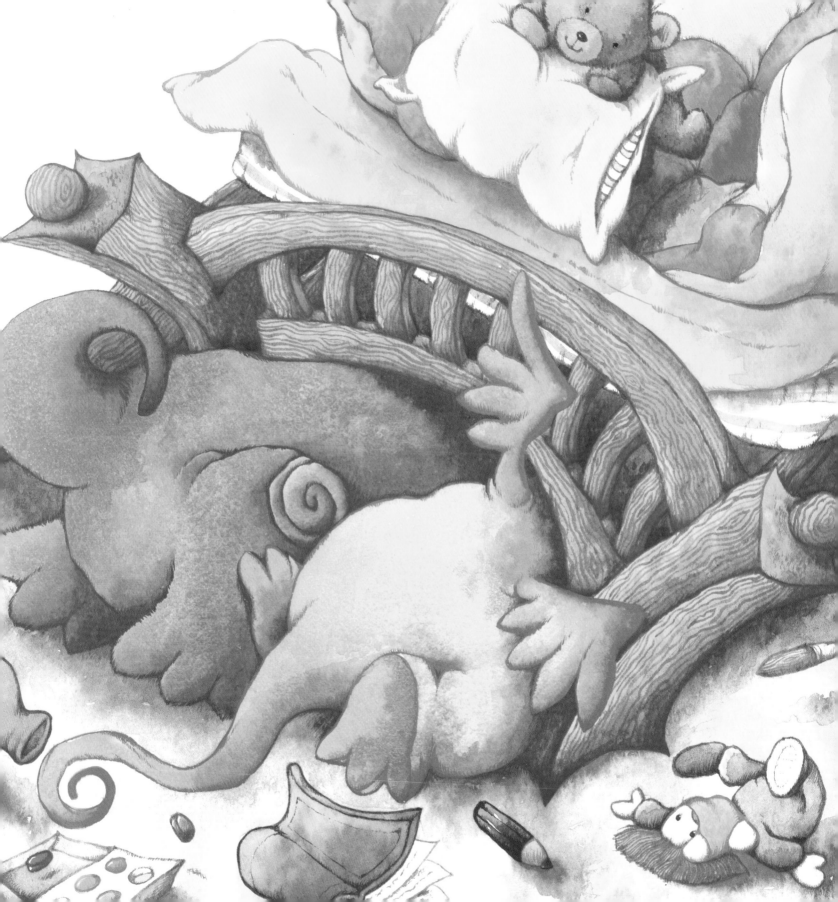

Now I tidy my room,
Every nook,
  every crack.

I want to make sure
That they **never**
come back!

For Daniel, Nicholas and Sadie

First published in 2004
by Meadowside Children's Books
185 Fleet Street, London EC4A 2HS

Text © Beth Shoshan, 2004
Illustrations © Piers Harper, 2004

A CIP catalogue record for this book
is available from the British Library.
Printed in India

10 9 8 7 6 5 4 3 2 1